Basic Karate

Basic Karate

by E. G. BARTLETT

faber and faber

LONDON · BOSTON

First published in 1980
by Faber and Faber Limited
3 Queen Square London WC1N 3AU
Reprinted 1982 and 1984

Printed in Great Britain by
Whitstable Litho Ltd
Whitstable, Kent
All rights reserved

British Library Cataloguing in Publication Data
Bartlett, Eric George
  Basic karate.
  1. Karate
  I. Title
  796.8'153   GV1114.3
ISBN 0-571-11435-0
ISBN 0-571-11436-9Pbk

Contents

Acknowledgements

The author wishes to thank Paul Jordan and Raymond Williams for help in demonstrating the movements in this book, Jerry Coughlan for help at an earlier stage, and Mr. K. Newman of Hylton Warner & Co., Ltd., who took the photographs.

Introduction

Karate is fast overtaking judo in popularity among the oriental fighting arts being practised in the West. The earlier Chinese art of Kung Fu, on which karate is partly based, is also becoming more widely practised.

Literally 'karate' means 'empty hands'. It is a system of fighting without weapons. Okinawa can claim credit for playing the greatest part in the development of karate but, of course, there was simultaneous development of methods of fighting without weapons throughout the world.

Boxing and wrestling have been known in Europe since the days of Rome's greatness. They probably spread from Europe to India and thence to Thailand, where the Thai form of boxing with hands and feet still persists, rather like the French *savate*.

The Chinese systems of fighting, known variously as Chu'an Fa, Kempo and Kung Fu, originated from the teaching of the Indian Buddhist monk, Daruma Taishi, who went to China in the sixth century to teach Buddhism to the Emperor.

He stayed at the Shaolin-szu monastery and the discipline he demanded of his students was so severe that it proved too much for many of them physically. To improve their stamina and general health, he began teaching them what is now known as 'Shaolin Temple Boxing'. His system was so effective as a means of self-defence that his pupils soon became renowned for their fighting abilities.

Chinese wrestling, which was called 'Chiao Ti Shu' was known as long ago as the seventh century BC. It was a popular sport with the people. Kempo developed from this. In the sixteenth century the Chinese general, Ch'I Chi-Kuang, combined the fist-fighting arts known in China and systematized them into a school of fighting. With the advent of firearms, this system of fighting came to be prized more as an aid to physical fitness than for its actual use in war.

What is known as 'Kung Fu' in the West today originated from these ancient arts. There are many schools, each giving emphasis to their particular styles. Thus one school recommends evading the opponent's attacks so that they pass by and leave you free to retaliate; another recommends blocking techniques.

Simultaneously with this development and systematization of the fist-fighting arts in China there was a development of similar arts in Okinawa. From the twelfth century and earlier there had been extensive trade between Okinawa and China and knowledge of the Chinese arts was brought over. In the fifteenth century King Hashi united all the Ryukyu Islands into one kingdom, and to ensure rule by law, he banned the use of weapons. This led to the first serious study by the people of Okinawa of methods of unarmed combat. Two hundred years later, under the rule of the Satsuma clan, weapons were banned for the second time and the study again became necessary.

The various movements—blocks, blows, chops, kicks, etc.—were brought together into a system by Funakoshi Gichin, who is regarded as the founder of modern karate. He was born in 1869 in Shuri, Okinawa, and began his studies at the age of eleven. By the time he was an adult he was developing his own system based on the best techniques he had learnt from other masters. In this way he did for karate what Dr Jigoro Kano was to do for judo in Japan.

Japan had its own fighting arts. Sumo wrestling was known earlier than the third century BC and what was practised as sumo then was not much like the national sport of that name today. Kicks and blows were allowed so we should think of sumo as wrestling with no holds barred. The rules that govern sumo as a sport today only began to be used in the Naro period when the fighting art became a sport. Ju-jutsu schools were also native to Japan. There were many of these teaching not only the throws and wrestling movements that we associate with modern judo, but also blows and kicks. These attacks on vital spots formed a separate branch of the art, known as 'atemi-waza'.

Funakoshi Gichin introduced his system of karate into Japan in 1917 and returned to lecture and teach there in 1922. The Japanese had always been skilled at adapting arts that were not indigenous to their country and absorbing them into their own culture. They combined Funakoshi's karate with some of their own atemi-waza and ju-jutsu, and the resultant amalgam formed the basis of modern karate.

In 1948 the Japanese Karate Association was founded. Funakoshi became its Chief Instructor. From that time on, the development of karate as a sport was rapid. Funakoshi died in 1957 at the age of eighty-eight.

There are many schools of karate in Japan. The principal ones are the Shotokan School—which was Funakoshi's own—the Wado School, the Shito School and the Goju School. In 1964 these combined to form the All Japan Karate Association.

Karate first came to Europe in the 1950s. Undoubtedly its popularity owes much to the pioneer work of H. D. Plée of Paris, who introduced the sport into France. He remembers that 'Napoleon had an inquiry made about Karate in 1809'. But the art had to wait another 150 years before it became at all well known in Europe.

It is probably only since the early 1960s that karate has begun to achieve popularity in Britain. It follows the earlier development of judo. Both karate and judo are quite popular in the United States. The Americans are fortunate in having more Japanese masters resident there to assist them in their studies. The highest-graded master at present in Europe is Tatsuo Suzuki.

In Europe, in the United States

and in Britain tournaments are now held regularly for students of karate and it is likely that one day it will be one of the sports included in the Olympic Games. Some Japanese masters have expressed the fear that this concentration on karate as a competitive sport may lead it to go the same way as judo and the finer points and philosophy behind the study be lost in mere desire to win.

In this book we are going to look at the philosophy and the basic ideas behind karate before proceeding to a study of the stances, the blows, the chops, the kicks, the blocks and all the other movements. We shall study one of the commoner katas, look at training methods and study contest rules. We shall also see how karate can be applied to self-defence, although it must be stressed that this is not one of the primary objects of study.

First, let us rid ourselves of some misconceptions. As part of a public display, karate experts will sometimes break a plank of wood or smash a pile of roofing tiles with a vicious blow or kick, which has given the impression that this is what karate is all about. Nothing could be further from the truth. Anyone can learn to do these tricks in six months with a little practice and with faith. Karate is much more difficult. It requires anatomical knowledge; it demands long and patient practice to develop accuracy and speed of attack; it calls for a moral and spiritual development.

The study can be followed purely for its physical and mental benefits or with a view to taking part in competition. For whichever reason the student takes part, he is bound to benefit in all ways.

1. Basic Principles

Karate is an application of simple scientific principles to the art of attack and defence. The first one we should think about is:

$$\text{Force} = \text{Mass} \times \text{Velocity}^2$$

This means that you must use the whole weight of your body when punching or kicking and your fist or foot must be at its maximum speed at the moment of impact.

Punches are not thrown from the shoulder as in boxing. A firm balanced stance is important, with the rear leg pressed hard to the floor. The movement originates at the hip. The arm is straight at the moment of impact.

The second principle is:

To every action there is an equal and opposite reaction.

As your right arm goes forward in a punch, your left is brought sharply back. This will be described in greater detail when we deal with punching. It is sufficient to note here that the withdrawing of the opposite arm creates a reaction force which adds to the power of the punch. Furthermore, when the fist strikes, the force passes back along the arm, down the rear leg to the floor and is reflected back again along the leg and arm to add more force to the punch.

The third principle is:

The shorter the time a striking force is applied, the more effective it is.

Speed of hitting and of withdrawing the fist after impact is therefore vital.

The fourth principle is:

The smaller the striking area the greater will be the force.

This can be seen if you compare striking with the fingers in the abdomen compared with striking with the fist. Try it gently on yourself: your fist is a big area and will not go in so far. The force is diffused over a bigger area of your abdomen. If you wear a boxing glove, the force is diffused even more. A blow with a glove hurts less than a blow with bare knuckles. A jab with your fingertips hurts most of all because it penetrates and is concentrated on one small area.

The fifth principle is:

Inhaling relaxes the muscles, exhaling contracts them.

You must breathe out when you hit. This leads to the shout that some karate students give at the moment of hitting. It not only helps them to concentrate all their force, but the actual expulsion of breath tightens up their muscles. Have you ever seen a gang of workmen on the railway lifting a heavy rail? The ganger will shout 'Heigh-up', and his men will join in the shout as they concentrate all their forces together.

The singing of sea shanties by sailors in days of sail was for the same purpose specifically, to enable the men to concentrate all their efforts for heavy tasks such as raising the anchor or the mainsail.

Taking these five principles into consideration—hitting with your whole body, withdrawing the opposite fist as you strike, hitting as fast as possible, hitting with the smallest possible area, and breathing out as you hit—this is called 'focusing' your punch.

It is most important. A punch must be focused and it must be delivered from a position of strong balance. If you are off-balance yourself, your punch is weakened.

As in judo, the karate student must learn to relax when he is fighting. Tension makes it impossible to adapt quickly to new situations. Tension prepares you to meet the attack you are expecting, but it does not allow you to change your stance rapidly to meet another unexpected attack. You must watch your opponent at all times. Keep your eyes on him, but do not necessarily look him in the eyes. Try to have all his body in your field of vision.

Fear and anger produce tension, which mars your fighting ability. Train hard so that you do not need to be afraid of any man. Do not be angry whatever happens. One of the meanings of 'karate' is 'empty hands' as we have learnt, but this does not mean just empty of weapons. It means with the mind empty of evil intent and with the spirit empty of hate.

To succeed in karate you must train hard. Often you will find the repetition of exercises boring and the postures you are asked to assume will make your limbs

ache. You must fight your desire to give up through boredom or discomfort. My own master told me: 'It is like fighting yourself. If you cannot fight yourself, you will never fight anyone else.' Think about this when you are tempted to give up your training because of the weakness of your own flesh.

One of the teachings of Zen is that the mind you are born with is pure, and that it only becomes soiled through contact with the world. You do not have fear and hate when you are born. You acquire these characteristics. One of the aims of karate training is to enable you to recover this lost innocence.

Karate is practised on any level surface that will not injure the feet. It is practised bare-footed like judo. A gymnasium is a satisfactory place if the floor is not too slippery. Often judo clubs that run karate courses allow students to practise on the judo mat. This is an admirable surface, as it permits throwing movements to be practised, which are rather dangerous on a wooden floor.

Students wear a white cotton suit, rather like a judo suit, except that the jacket is not quite as long, and the material is not as strong because it does not have to stand up to the strains of pulling. The karate jacket reaches just below the waist and the two parts of the jacket are tied together, either with a tape inside the front or with tapes at the sides. A belt is worn round the waist and tied in front in a reef knot so as to hold the jacket more firmly around you. There are no buttons or buckles on jacket or trousers to cause injury. The trousers come to the ankles. The whole suit is made of a crisp white cotton, which gives a cracking sound when you make a sharp movement.

No blows are actually landed in karate of course. It would be terribly dangerous to land any of the punches, kicks or chops described later in this book. The student must have sufficient self-control and judgement of distance to be able to 'pull' his punches a fraction of an inch from their target. For this reason beginners are not normally allowed to take part in free practice. They usually spend their time learning to control their own movements without actually facing a partner until they have reached a sufficient degree of mastery over themselves.

Training sessions usually begin with a few warming-up exercises. Movements are learnt as 'standing movements', the class performing them together like soldiers on a parade ground, without facing a partner at all. Later, movements are practised on the move, for example, moving forward down the room and punching with alternate hands on each step. In this form of practice, importance is attached to correct carriage of the body and to balance.

Following some months of this type of practice, students progress to the kumites. These are pre-arranged movements practised with a partner. A blow by one is blocked and countered by the other. Only after much practice of the kumites is free or semi-free practice allowed. Contest should not be indulged in by beginners. As in judo, knowledge of karate is preserved in ritual sequences of movements known as 'katas'. We shall be studying an example later in the book.

As we have mentioned in the introduction, there are different schools of karate. Some teach tension of the muscles to a greater degree than others. Some teach their students to harden their hands by chopping at wood or bricks. Other schools prefer their students to concentrate on speed and accuracy of attack. It is certain that mere hardness of hand or foot is useless without the speed and skill to land a blow on the right spot.

As in all Japanese sports, there are grades of ability. These are awarded partly for knowledge and demonstration of movements and partly for contest. The belt which secures the jacket is coloured to denote the grade of the wearer.

The 8th, 7th, 6th, 5th and 4th Kyus are classed as beginners and wear a white belt. The 3rd, 2nd and 1st Kyus are classed as intermediate grades and wear a brown belt. All the Dan grades are masters and wear a black belt. In some of the Western countries, this division of grades is varied and the number of Kyu grades is six, as in judo. When this is done, the students usually wear white belt for 6th Kyu, yellow for 5th, orange for 4th, green for 3rd, blue for 2nd and brown for 1st, as in judo.

Great stress is laid upon courtesy to one's master and to one's practice partners and to opponents in a contest. This is shown partly by cleanliness of attire and person, but also by politeness of manner and by the formal bows or salutations.

At the beginning of a training session the class makes the kneeling bow known as 'rei' to the master. He and they kneel down together, the master facing the class, and they salute each other in the following manner:

Kneel with the feet turned back so that the tops of the toes and the insteps are in contact with the floor. Cross the big toes. Bend the body forward and place both forearms on the ground so that the elbows are under the shoulders and the forearms point inward at an angle of about forty-five degrees. The hands should be a few inches apart, palms flat on the ground. From this position, lower the head so that the top of the skull is shown to the partner. See Fig. 1.

Fig 2

Fig 1

This salutation and the standing one which follows should always be made with due thought to its meaning and with dignity and truth.

The standing salutation is made, before and after practice, to one's individual partner. It is also made before and after contest, both to one's opponent and to the referee. It would normally be made in a class to the master if the student asked a question, or if the master called him forward for any purpose. The standing bow is made in the following manner:

Stand upright about six feet from the partner, hands at sides, palms against the side of the trouser legs. Bend forward slightly from the waist, lowering the head so that the skull is presented to the partner. Let the hands slide down the sides of the legs as you bow. See Fig. 2.

Note that the bow is very slight, not deep, and that the body does not come forward more than fifteen degrees from the vertical.

Some schools teach their students to make the standing bow with their fists clenched as in the Open Leg Stance (Hachiji Dachi) described in Chapter 3. This is not general practice, however, and it seems to me that the bow as described above is more in keeping with its purpose, since it is made from a position of repose and not from a 'ready' or 'fighting' stance.

2. Warming-up Exercises

The object of warming-up exercises is simply to tone up the muscles and to loosen oneself up, preparatory to the karate training session. The following sequence of exercises will be found helpful for these purposes. Do them at the beginning and end of every training session.

1. DEEP KNEE BENDS

Stand upright, hands at sides. Bend the knees as far as possible, swinging the arms forward to the position where they are straight out in front of you and level with the chest. Breathe in as you go down and out as you come up. If you can keep your heels on the ground when doing this exercise, it will help to loosen up your ankle joints and make them more flexible, but if you find this impossible in the beginning leave it until you are more advanced. Repeat ten times.

2. KNEES ROTATING

Stand upright, feet together. Bend forward and place the palms of your hands on your knees. Now, bending the knees slightly, move them around in a circular motion, first clockwise, and then anti-clockwise. Repeat ten times each way.

3. HEAD ROTATING

Bend the head forward, take it to your left, take it upright, then back, to the right, then forward again, moving it round and round in a rotary motion. Place your hands on your hips while performing this exercise. Repeat ten times clockwise, and then a further ten anti-clockwise.

4. SIDE BENDS

Stand with the feet astride. Bend to your left, letting your left palm slide down the side of your leg and taking your right arm up in the air, fingers pointing over your head to your left. Straighten up and reverse the exercise by bending to your right. Repeat ten times each side.

5. TRUNK TURNING

Stand with the feet astride. Raise arms sideways to shoulder level. Now swing the trunk round from the hips as far as you can to your left, letting the head turn as well. Swing back and round to your right. Repeat ten times each side.

6. FORWARD BEND AND BACK STRETCH

Stand with the feet apart. Bend forward to touch the floor with the hands, being careful not to bend the knees. From this position, straighten up and lean back as far as you can, letting your head go back as well and taking your arms above your head and back. Breathe in as you come up, and out as you go down. Repeat ten times.

7. SIT-UPS

Lie flat on your back, feet together. Either tuck your feet under a heavy object, to prevent them coming up, or get your partner to hold them down. Clasp your hands behind your head. Now sit up and pull your head forward with your hands as far as possible. Breathe out as you come up and in as you go back down.
Repeat ten times.

8. LEG RAISES

Lie on your back, arms at sides. Take both heels off the ground. Now slowly raise the right leg, lower it to just off the ground, then raise the left leg and lower that to just off the ground. The heels are not put back on the ground until the end.
Repeat ten times with each leg, raising them alternately.

9. WRIST TURNING

Sit cross-legged on the floor. Take the right fingers in the left hand and gently rotate the right hand on the wrist joint in a circular motion. Rotate first clockwise and then anti-clockwise. Repeat the exercise with the left wrist.
Repeat ten times each way with each hand.

10. ANKLE TURNING

Still sitting, take the right foot in the left hand and gently rotate it on the ankle joint, first clockwise and then anti-clockwise. Repeat the exercise with the left foot in the right hand.
Repeat ten times with each foot.

11. LEG STRETCHING

Stand with feet apart. Now deeply bend the right knee and stretch out the left leg sideways. Bend forward and with both hands press down on the left knee joint so as to stretch the leg. Repeat with the left knee bent and the right leg stretched out sideways.
Repeat ten times with each leg.

12. CYCLING ON BACK

Lie on your back. Swing both legs up in the air and over your head, supporting yourself by putting the palms of your hands under your buttocks and your elbows on the ground. In this position perform a cycling motion with your legs.
Do this for one minute.

13. LEG AND ARM RELAXING

Stand upright. Let the arms hang loosely and shake them, being sure to let the wrists hang loosely as well and not to tense them. Raise each leg off the ground in turn and shake it gently, being sure to relax all the muscles and to let it hang from the hip joint. There is no set time or number of repetitions for this relaxing process, but about one minute should be sufficient.

Do not be disappointed or misled by the very simple nature of these exercises, and do not omit them as unnecessary to your training programme. Top experts use them to condition their bodies for the harder training that is to follow.

3. Basic Stances

Stance is very important in karate. You must be on balance so that an attack will not knock you over. You must be able to move freely from one stance into another. You must vary your stance according to the attack or defence you are making.

We shall look at six basic stances. There are others, but you will find that they are simply variations on these six.

1. THE OPEN LEG STANCE (HACHIJI DACHI)

Stand with the legs shoulder-width apart, toes pointing slightly outward. Clench the fists and hold them at the ready position just in front of your thighs. Keep your legs straight and your body upright. Look straight ahead of you. Relax your body so that you will be able to move rapidly from this ready stance into any other. See Fig. 3.

2. THE STRADDLE LEG STANCE (KIBA DACHI)

Spread your legs about twice the width of your shoulders. Keep the heels on the ground and point the toes directly forward. Now lower your body, keeping it upright, bending your knees so that they come directly over your big toes. Keep your body upright and look straight ahead. Push your chest out. Clench your fists and hold them in front of you at the ready, as in the first stance. See Fig. 4.

FIG 3

FIG 4

3. THE FORWARD STANCE (ZENKUTSU DACHI)

From the Open Leg Stance (No. 1), move your right leg forward about twice the width of your shoulders. Bend the knee so that it comes directly over the big toe. Keep your body upright, look straight ahead, and extend your back leg so that it is straight, with the toes pointing forward. The front leg bears about three-fifths of the weight, the rear leg two-fifths. Clench the fists. Take the left fist back on to the left hip and hold the right one straight out in front of you and about two inches above your right thigh. The back of the right fist is upward, but the left is turned so that the back of the fist is downward. See Fig. 5.

4. THE BACK STANCE (KOKUTSU DACHI)

From the Open Leg Stance (No. 1), turn the right foot to point outward to your right side and move the left foot forward to about twice the width of your shoulders, as in the last movement. Your right knee is bent to come over your right big toe and your left knee is slightly bent. Face directly to your front. Your rear leg must support about seventy per cent of your weight because this stance is used to enable you to raise the front leg off the ground for kicks and blocks with the leg. See Fig. 6.

Note that in both this and the last stance, the stance can equally well be taken with either leg forward, simply by reversing all

FIG 5   FIG 6

FIG 7   FIG 8

the directions. In moving around for free practice in karate, you will find that you are constantly changing from the one stance to the other.

5. THE CAT STANCE (NEKO ASHI DACHI)

From the Open Leg Stance (No. 1), bend your right knee so that the knee is over the big toe. Raise the left foot and take it forward a pace with the knee bent over the toes and only the toes resting on the ground. Keep the right heel on the ground. It will be seen in this stance that the rear leg is bearing all the weight so that the front leg is free for kicking. See Fig. 7.

Again, although it has been described with the right leg to the rear, it can be performed with the left leg to the rear.

6. THE HOUR GLASS STANCE (SANCHIN DACHI)

From the Open Leg Stance (No. 1), take the right foot forward, half-turning to your left, and place the right foot on the ground, toes pointing inward. Swivel on your left foot at the same time so that the toes of that foot also point inward. Bend the knees inward so that they are over the big toes and so that you can bring them together quickly to foil an attack on the groin. Clench the fists and raise the hands in front of the body with the elbows close to the sides. See Fig. 8.

Again, this stance can be performed by taking the left foot forward and reversing all the directions.

The important thing in all these stances is that the body must be upright, you must keep your eyes on your opponent, and the hips must be lowered as much as possible. Karate is performed from a low posture.

A good exercise is to take up the Kiba Dachi Stance (No. 2) and try to remain in it for a few minutes at a time. Start with three minutes and work up to ten.

You will find that the knees begin to ache and you want to raise your body to relieve the discomfort. If you persist in the exercise, fighting your weakness, however, you will find it gradually becomes more bearable, your knee joints are strengthened and the self-discipline involved will make you a better karate man.

4. Postures and Movement

There are three basic postures in karate, but bear in mind that you are constantly changing posture and stance in making attacks and in defending.

1. THE FRONT FACING POSTURE

From the Open Leg Stance, the Straddle Leg Stance, the Forward Stance, the Back Stance, the Cat Stance or even the Hour Glass Stance, you can adopt the Front Facing Posture, though the last-named stance is more usually taken with a Side Facing Posture.

The main feature of the Front Facing Posture is that the top half of your body is squarely facing the opponent. Your body must be upright and not lean forward or to either side. See Fig. 9.

2. THE HALF FRONT FACING POSTURE

Take up the stance shown in the last posture. Now turn your trunk to make an angle of forty-five degrees to the opponent, without moving your feet. Again, remain upright, and keep your eyes on your opponent. See Fig. 10.

3. THE SIDE FACING POSTURE

This is generally taken from either the Straddle Leg Stance or the Hour Glass Stance.

Again, your body is upright, but your feet are on a line at right angles to a line drawn through your opponent's feet. Your side is towards him, but you look over your shoulder and keep your eyes on him. Your body must be upright. See Fig. 11.

FIG 9

FIG 10

FIG 11

You will readily see that the Front Facing Posture facilitates attacks with fist or foot and a turn into the Side Facing Posture or the Half Front Facing Posture could be one way of avoiding a straight punch or a kick aimed at yourself.

Let us now consider movement.

1. GENERAL POINTS ON MOVEMENT

You must be on balance at all times. You must move smoothly. You must try not to raise your hips in the slight up and down movement that you get in ordinary walking, but rather to slide the feet around, much as in judo, but not losing speed. Think of keeping the soles of the feet as near the ground as possible. Keep the body upright and keep the eyes on the opponent.

2. MOVING FORWARD

Take up the Back Stance (Kokutsu Dachi) as described in No. 4 of the last chapter. Keep the body front-facing. To move forward from here, simply bring the right foot forward, swivelling on the left, so that when the right comes as far in advance as it was previously behind your left foot is pointing to your left, outward, and bears seventy per cent of your weight, and your right is pointing to the front. As you are making this move, your hands also change position, and the left fist goes back on to the left hip as

FIG 12

FIG 13

the right makes the downward block. See Figs. 12 and 13.

3. MOVING BACKWARD

From the above position, to move backward, you simply take the right foot back to its original position, turning it as you go, and swivel on the rear foot. Your hands also change position again. In effect, you are simply reversing what you have just done.

5. TURNING

Consider a turn from the last position, that is from the Back Stance (Kokutsu Dachi), with your left foot forward, and your right fist on your hip. When you turn you must be prepared to defend, so you normally make a block as you turn, even in practice. Take up the posture. Now take your right hand from your hip up close to your left ear. See Fig. 14.

FIG 14

FIG 15

4. TSUGI ASHI

As well as moving by crossing the legs in the manner described above, you can move with the Tsugi Ashi steps used in judo. In this, you first move one foot in any direction and then bring the other nearly up to it but without passing it. Then move the first foot again and bring the other nearly up to it without passing, so progressing in any desired direction.

Do an about-turn to your right by simply swivelling on your feet, so that your left foot now points to the side and bears seventy per cent of the weight and your right is pointing forward. As you turn, make a Downward Block (Gedan Barai) with your right hand and bring your left back on to your left hip ready for an attack. See Fig. 15.

The blocks and punches are more fully described in the chapters which follow. For the moment simply follow the diagrams.

To practise movement, take up the Back Stance with the left foot forward and change it to the right foot forward, then again to the left foot forward, letting the hands change with the feet, and so progress down the room. If, when you reach the end, your left foot is forward, do a right-about-turn; if your right foot is forward, do a left-about-turn. Having turned, go back down the room the other way and turn again to come back up. Think all the time of not raising your hips. It will help if you look at a point level with your eyes and con-centrate on moving towards it.

When crossing the feet in these movements, do not part them widely. At all times they must be the natural distance apart in a sideways direction although, in a back-to-front direction, they are, of course, more widely spaced. It will help to think of your feet moving forward on parallel lines which are the same distance apart as your shoulders. Keeping the feet thus enables you to bring your knees together quickly if you need to block attacks on your groin.

To practise moving backward, start in the Back Stance and bring the front foot back, changing hands, as described in No. 3 above. Go back another step and then another until you reach the end of the room. Then come forward again.

Try to get used always to being on balance when you move. Beginners tend to lean over or to raise their bodies. Do the moves slowly and smoothly to begin with and only speed them up when you achieve accuracy.

5. Striking Points and Targets

In this chapter we shall study the targets that are attacked in karate and then give a simple list of those parts of your own body that are used in making the attacks. How the attacks are made will be dealt with in the chapters which follow. Here, we shall simply indicate which striking points are used against which targets. Consult Figs. 16 and 17 for the exact location of the targets.

TARGETS OF ATTACK

1. THE CENTRE OF THE SKULL

The point is the middle of the skull. The effect is concussion.

2. THE TEMPLE

On either side of the face, just about level with the corner of the eye and about half-way between the eye and the ear is the point of attack. A severe blow here can cause internal bleeding and death.

3. THE BRIDGE OF THE NOSE

Just at the top of the nose, between the eyes, is a slight hollow. A blow in this is very dangerous and can cause death.

4. THE EYES

No explanation is needed. The effect of attack is obvious.

FIG 16

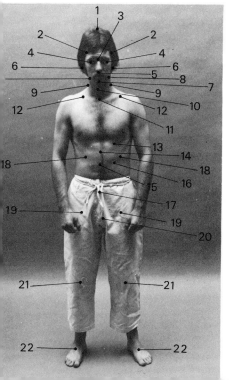

FIG 17

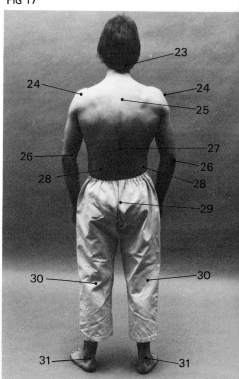

5. THE BASE OF THE NOSE

The attack is made at an angle of forty-five degrees upward and backward. It is very dangerous.

6. THE HOLLOWS BEHIND THE EARS

Pressure here is very painful and will cause loss of consciousness.

7. THE CHIN

A blow on the point can cause loss of consciousness.

8. THE JAW

The lower jaw bones extend along the bottom of the face. The points of attack are just to the side of the chin.

9. THE SIDES OF THE NECK

The points of attack are the carotid arteries, which run up the sides of the neck carrying blood to the brain. They are best attacked rather low down on the neck.

10. THE ADAM'S APPLE

This is the prominent cartilage of the larynx, seen as a lump in the front of the throat.

11. THE HOLLOW AT THE BASE OF THE THROAT

You can easily find this on yourself and test its vulnerability.

12. THE CLAVICLES

These are the bones extending from the tip of the shoulder to the breastbone. There is one on each side. They are easily snapped by a direct blow or by a blow inward on the point of the shoulder.

13. THE HEART

This is under the breastbone and rather more to the left than the right. Blows under it will slow a man down.

14. THE SOLAR PLEXUS

This is the soft part of your body just below the breastbone. All the nervous systems of the lower abdomen meet here and it is therefore very sensitive.

15. THE STOMACH

This is about half-way between the solar plexus and the navel.

16. THE SPLEEN

This is to the left of the stomach.

17. THE BLADDER

This is much lower than the navel, just above where the penis joins the body. The area above the bladder is a point of attack.

18. THE SIDE RIBS

It is the bottom pair, the so-called floating ribs that are usually attacked, but any attack in the ribs is painful.

19. THE GROIN

The vulnerable points are to be found in the front of the body about half-way across. They are pressure points in first aid because they are the points at which the arteries are near the surface of the skin.

20. THE TESTICLES

Damage to these is very serious and can lead to death.

21. THE KNEE-CAPS

These are the bones at the front of the knees. A blow here may smash them or may lead to cartilage trouble.

22. THE INSTEPS

These are on top of the foot. The

bones can be crushed by stamping on this area.

23. THE BASE OF THE SKULL

The point of attack is at the back, just below the protective skull bone. The blow is commonly called a rabbit punch.

24. THE TIPS OF THE SHOULDERS

Blows here made inward and downward will fracture the clavicles.

25. THE TOP OF THE BACK

The point is midway between the shoulder-blades.

26. THE ELBOWS

Blows on the back of the elbows may dislocate or fracture the joint.

27. THE MIDDLE OF THE BACK

The point of attack is at belt level in the backbone.

28. THE KIDNEYS

These are situated to left and right of the spine, just above the waist. You can easily find them on yourself by gently pressing in until you discover the point that hurts most.

29. THE BASE OF THE SPINE

The point of attack is the coccyx, which is a rudimentary tail. A blow here can cause sickness.

30. THE KNEES

The hollows at the back of the knees are sensitive.

31. THE ACHILLES TENDONS

These are the tendons at the back of the heels.

From what has been said briefly above, it will be realized why blows must never be landed in karate and why students must have a sufficient sense of responsibility never to use their art outside their halls of practice. The highest standards of behaviour are demanded of students and any misuse of their art would result in expulsion from any properly conducted school.

In some schools masters will allow their pupils to land the blows with only a fraction of their true force, but the general custom is never to land any blow or kick at all. If you depart from this practice, it should only be with the consent of your master and your partner, and with the greatest care not to injure the partner.

Students are not generally allowed to face a partner, even in practice, until they have attained sufficient skill to pull their punches instead of landing them. This requires very accurate judgement of distance and timing, and an almost instinctive knowledge of what your partner is likely to do, so that he does not of himself move into your blow.

Although blows may not be landed, they must be aimed correctly. This accuracy is one of the things that will gain points in competition or in grading examination. In every respect, a blow must be directed and focused as if it were intended to take full effect, but the student must have so judged his distance from his partner that the blow stops a fraction of an inch short of the target.

At this stage of your study, learn to identify the precise targets, first on your own body, and then on the body of your partner. This will teach you which points you have to protect on yourself, and which points you have to aim for in your attacks.

STRIKING POINTS

The term 'striking points' is given to those parts of your own body which are used in making attacks. There are twenty.

1. THE FIRST TWO KNUCKLES OF THE FIST

Used against the bridge of the nose, the temples, the jaw, the chin, the upper back, the solar plexus, the floating ribs, the lower back, the kidneys, the abdomen, the testicles, the base of the nose, the Adam's apple, the stomach, the spleen, the heart.

2. THE BACK OF THE CLENCHED FIST

Used against the bridge of the nose, the bottom of the nose, the solar plexus, the kidneys, the floating ribs, the testicles.

3. THE BOTTOM OF THE CLENCHED FIST

The side opposite the thumb is used against the skull, the clavicles, the floating ribs, the tips of the shoulders.

4. THE SECOND KNUCKLE OF THE SECOND FINGER

Used between the eyes, at the base of the nose, against the Adam's apple, the solar plexus, the kidneys, behind the ears, at the groin.

5. THE SECOND KNUCKLES OF THE HAND

Used at the base of the nose, the throat, the temples, the side of the neck.

6. THE OPEN HANDS

Used to attack the ears.

7. THE V BETWEEN THE FINGERS AND THE THUMB

Used to attack the Adam's apple.

8. THE FIRST TWO FINGERS SPREAD APART

Used to attack the eyes.

9. THE FIRST FINGER

Used to attack the eyes or the solar plexus.

10. THE LITTLE FINGER EDGE OF THE HAND

Used to attack the temples, the ribs, the throat, the sides of the neck, the kidneys.

11. THE FIRST THREE FINGERS

Used to attack the solar plexus, the ribs, the throat, the testicles.

12. THE HEEL OF THE PALM

Used to attack the jaw, the base of the nose, the solar plexus, the testicles.

13. THE CURVE OF THE WRIST

Used to attack the collar bone.

14. THE ELBOW

Used to attack the ribs, the chin, the solar plexus, the kidneys.

15. THE KNEE

Used to attack the face, the solar plexus, the heart, the spleen, the testicles, the abdomen, the coccyx.

16. THE INSTEP

Used to attack the testicles.

17. THE FOOT EDGE

Used to attack the knees, the shin bones, the solar plexus, the armpits, the floating ribs, behind the knees.

18. THE SOLE OF THE FOOT

Used against the instep and the solar plexus.

19. THE HEEL

Used against the jaw, the solar plexus, the testicles, the insteps.

20. THE BALL OF THE FOOT

Used against the face, the solar plexus, the testicles, the ribs, the body generally.

It will be realized that this list is not complete. It simply indicates the usual attacks that are made with these striking points. In general, any striking point can be used against any target, but some targets are small and these are best attacked by a small striking point. For example, the fist will not reach the hollow at the top of the nose, but the one knuckle of the finger will.

We shall study details of how these attacks are made in the next two chapters.

6. Blows and Strikes

In karate, 'blows' are what would be commonly called 'punches' or 'kicks', and 'strikes' are what would be commonly called 'chops' whether given with the hand or foot. In this chapter we shall be studying attacks with the hand or arm.

First, it is important to learn how to clench the fist correctly. It must be very tightly closed with no space inside. Beginning with the little finger, bend the fingers in as high as possible up the palm. Then bend the fingers over so that the first knuckles are in contact with the palm. Lock them in this position by bending the thumb inwards over the first and second finger. The back of the wrist must form a straight line with your forearm. You should be able to put a ruler along the back of your hand and up your forearm and find it is a straight line. If the wrist is bent at all, either way, you will risk injury to it when you hit.

We should first distinguish between two basic types of punch: the reverse punch and the lunge punch.

THE REVERSE PUNCH

Take up the Forward Stance (Zenkutsu Dachi) as described in Chapter 3, No. 3, having the body facing directly forward in the Front Facing Posture described in Chapter 4, No. 1. Have the right foot forward. Now, the right hand with fist clenched is held straight out in front of you, palm down, with the fist about two inches above the thigh, and the left hand is held on your left hip, with palm upward, also with the fist clenched. The reverse punch is so called because it is made with the fist that is on the same side as the rear leg. In this case it is the left.

Strike straight, aiming at an imaginary opponent. The arm must shoot straight forward, the elbow brushing the side as it goes. When you land the punch, twist the wrist at the last moment so that the palm is turned down and the knuckles up at the moment of impact. This twisting action drives the punch home, rather like a screw being twisted in. As you punch with the left hand, so you must simultaneously withdraw your right hand on to your right hip, turning it at the last moment so that the palm is upward, ready for the next punch. Breathe out as you punch and make the expiration of breath into a sharp cry. See Fig. 18.

THE LUNGE PUNCH

Take up the same stance as above. The lunge punch is so called because you step forward as you punch, so the fist that strikes is then on the same side as the leg that is forward at the moment of impact. All that you do is to step forward with the

FIG 18   FIG 19

right foot at the same time as you punch, moving as described in Chapter 4, No. 2 of the section on movement. Remember to keep the punching arm straight with the elbow brushing the side, to bring the left hand back as you punch with the right and to twist both hands at the moment of impact. The two arm movements must be absolutely simultaneous. See Fig. 19.

Note that the terms 'reverse punch' and 'lunge punch' are general terms that apply to all the attacks listed in this chapter. If the foot on the same side as the attacking arm is to the rear, the punch is a reverse punch; if the foot on the same side advances as you punch so that it is forward at the moment of impact, the punch is a lunge punch.

SHORT RANGE PUNCHES

We have described above how you twist the fist at the moment of impact to add force to the

blow. If you are very close to your opponent, however, you can make any of the punches without this twist and they are then known as 'short range punches'. They are not quite so effective because the penetration generated by the twist is lost.

We shall now look in detail at each of the striking points listed in the last chapter and give some examples of attacks using each in turn.

1. ATTACKS WITH THE FIRST TWO KNUCKLES OF THE CLENCHED FIST (SEIKEN)

Clench the fist as described above. The attacking point is the first two knuckles. See Fig. 20. You will see that the attacking area is small and concentrates the force. We shall study six attacks with this.

(a) At the Bridge of the Nose

From the Back Stance (Kokutsu Dachi) and Front Facing Posture, as described in Chapter 3, No. 4, make a lunge punch as described

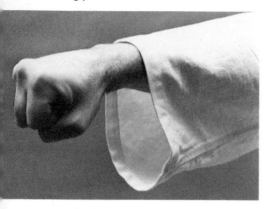

FIG 20

above, remembering to twist the wrist as the blow lands. Aim at the exact target, as indicated in Fig. 16.

In all blows you must think not just of hitting the opponent, but of hitting through him. A blow that is landed on the surface is not going to hurt. It must smash right through him. This is the basis of the karate trick of breaking a plank of wood. You hit not at the surface, but at a point the other side.

Of course, in practice you must never land a blow, so choose a distance from your practice partner to allow you to hit with the intent and power described, but still far enough away for the blow to fall just short. See Fig. 21.

(b) At the Temple

Take up the Open Leg Stance (Hachiji Dachi) described in Chapter 3, No. 1, with your left fist forward and your right on your hip. Move to your opponent's right-hand side by moving first your left foot and then your right, and deliver the punch to his right temple with your right fist as you do so. Remember that as the right hand punches, the left is withdrawn to the hip to increase the power of the blow. See Fig. 22.

(c) At the Jaw

Take up the Open Leg Stance as in the last movement and move to your opponent's left side, with right foot first, then left. Deliver a right-handed punch to the left side of his jaw. See Fig. 23.

FIG 21   FIG 22

Fig 23

Fig 24

(d) At the Heart
Take up the Back Stance as in example (a). Make a right-handed lunge punch at his heart. See Fig. 24.

(e) At the Stomach
From the Forward Stance (Zenkutsu Dachi), make a right-handed lunge punch at his stomach, moving your right foot

forward as you punch and remembering to twist the fist on impact. See Fig. 25.

(f) At the Middle of the Back
Opportunity for this would occur if you were able to move quickly behind your opponent, or if he turned his back on you. Attack at belt level with a right-handed lunge punch. See Fig. 26.

Fig 25

Fig 26

FIG 27

2. ATTACKS WITH THE BACK OF THE CLENCHED FIST (RIKEN)

Clench the fist as already described. The striking point is the flat of the back of the hand, particularly the area behind the first two knuckles. See Fig. 27.

We shall study five attacks with this.

(a) At the Base of the Nose

From the Open Leg Stance (Hachiji Dachi) facing your opponent, take your right foot forward, and swivel on your left into a Side Facing Posture and the Hour Glass Stance (Sanchin Dachi) described in Chapter 3, No. 6. Your right side is facing your opponent now. Use the back of the right fist to attack the base of his nose (the philtrum). As you strike with your right hand, bring your left back on to your left hip, palm upward. See Fig. 28.

(b) At the Solar Plexus

Move to your opponent's left side, facing the same way as he is, by stepping in with your right foot and swivelling on it to take your left back on to the same line. From the Open Leg Stance (Hachiji Dachi) use the back of your right hand to strike the opponent in the solar plexus. As you strike with your right, your left comes back on to your left hip, palm upward. See Fig. 29.

(c) At the Kidneys

Step in from the basic Open Leg Stance (Hachiji Dachi) by taking

FIG 28 FIG 29

Fig 30

Fig 31

your left foot forward on to the line of your opponent's feet and then bringing the right leg on to

Fig 32

the same line. Move into the Straddle Leg Stance (Kiba Dachi) described in Chapter 3, No. 2, as you do so. Strike him in the right kidney with the back of your right fist, bringing the left back on to your left hip, palm upward, as you do so. See Fig. 30.

(d) At the Spleen

As in the attack for the solar plexus (b), this is done from the side, facing the same way as your opponent. Move into it as for the earlier attack, but this time aim at his spleen. See Fig. 31.

(e) At the Base of the Skull

Move in as for the attack on the kidneys outlined in (c), but this time go a little farther behind your opponent and preserve the Open Leg Stance. Attack the base of his skull. Identify the target exactly in Fig. 17. See Fig. 32.

FIG 33

3. ATTACKS WITH THE BOTTOM OF THE CLENCHED FIST (TETTSUI)

Clench the fist as described earlier. The striking point is the area enclosed by a small circle around the side of the little finger and the muscle of the hand that you see bulging out when you clench your fist. See Fig. 33.

We shall study four attacks with this.

(a) At the Skull

This blow is rather like hammering, with your arm the hammer shaft and your fist the hammer head. From the Open Leg Stance (Hachiji Dachi), step forward with first left foot and then right, and deliver the blow directly down on your opponent's skull, bringing the left fist back on to your left hip as you hit, in the usual way. See Fig. 34.

(b) At the Clavicle

From the Open Leg Stance (Hachiji Dachi), step in as in the last movement and attack your opponent's left clavicle with your right fist, smashing it down on the bone and bringing your left fist back on to your left hip as usual. See Fig. 35.

FIG 34

FIG 35

Fig 36

Fig 37

(c) At the Floating Ribs

From the Open Leg Stance (Hachiji Dachi), move diagonally to your opponent's right side, by stepping forward with the right and swivelling on the left, so that you are in the Hour Glass Stance (Sanchin Dachi) and at an angle of forty-five degrees to his body. Make the blow at his right floating ribs with your right fist, at the same time bringing your left back on to your left hip, palm upward. See Fig. 36.

(d) At the Tips of the Shoulder

From the Open Leg Stance (Hachiji Dachi), step in with left foot, then right, to your opponent's side so that your feet are on a line with his. From this position strike the tip of his right shoulder with the bottom of your clenched right fist, bringing your left back on to your left hip as you do so. Strike in a sideways direction and slightly downward. See Fig. 37.

4. ATTACKS WITH THE SECOND KNUCKLE OF THE SECOND FINGER (IPPON KEN)

Clench your fist as described earlier and extend the second knuckle of the second finger, holding it tightly in position with the thumb. As will be seen, this is a small striking point, particularly suited to attacks where it has to be inserted into a small target area. See Fig. 38.

We shall study two attacks with this.

Fig 38

FIG 39   FIG 40

(a) At the Top of the Nose

The target is the little hollow between the eyes. From the Back Stance (Kokutsu Dachi), described in Chapter 3, No. 4, make a lunge punch with the right hand and deliver the blow with the one knuckle only. Bring the left hand back on to the left hip as usual. Twist the hands as you attack, in the usual way, so that the knuckle is screwed into the target. See Fig. 39.

(b) At the Solar Plexus

Proceed exactly as in the last movement, but this time attack the solar plexus. See Fig. 40.

5. ATTACKS WITH THE SECOND KNUCKLES OF THE HAND (HIRAKEN)

Do not clench your fist this time, but bend the fingers over on to the top of the palm so that the second knuckles form the front edge of the hand. These form a serrated line, curved rather like the edge of a shovel, and they are driven into the target as such a weapon would be. See Fig. 41.

We shall study three attacks with this.

FIG 41

FIG 42

FIG 43

FIG 44

(a) At the Base of the Nose

This wedge-shaped weapon is particularly suited for driving up at the base of the nose at a forty-five-degree angle. From the Back Stance (Kokutsu Dachi), make a lunge punch with your right hand. Twist the hand just before impact as usual and bring the opposite one back on to the left hip, twisting that also. See Fig. 42.

(b) At the Throat

The target this time is the Adam's apple. Proceed exactly as in the last movement, making a lunge punch with the right hand and bringing the left back. See Fig. 43.

(c) At the Temple

This attack is made when you are at your opponent's side, facing him diagonally, or if he is standing semi-facing to you. It can be made from the Open Leg Stance (Hachiji Dachi). Attack his left temple with your right fist, bringing your left back on to your left hip and twisting both as usual. See Fig. 44.

6. ATTACKS WITH THE OPEN HANDS (KUMADE)

The attacking area is really the palms of the hands. Bend the fingers in so that they touch their bases, the tops touching the palms. Bend the thumbs in and rest them on the palms, but without straining to put them farther in than they naturally lie. See Fig. 45.

FIG 46

The effect can be to shatter the ear drums if it is done violently. See Fig. 46.

7. ATTACK WITH THE V BETWEEN FINGERS AND THUMB (KOKO)

Slightly curve the fingers inwards and spread the thumb from the first finger widely. The attacking point is not the soft fold of skin between the thumb and fingers, but the muscle on the inside of

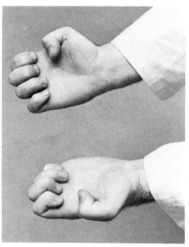

FIG 45

There is generally only one attack made with these striking points.

(a) The Ears

From the Open Leg Stance (Hachiji Dachi), simply step forward, left foot, then right, and clap your palms to your opponent's ears from the sides. The right goes to his left ear and the left to his right ear, of course.

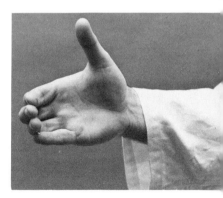

FIG 47

the base of the first finger. See Fig. 47.

Again, there is usually only one attack made with this striking point.

(a) The Adam's Apple

From the Back Stance (Kokutsu Dachi), make a lunge punch with your right hand at your opponent's Adam's apple, using

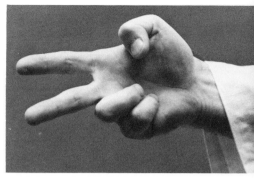

FIG 49

fingers into the palm. Bend the thumb into the palm. The two spread fingers are the attacking points. They can be toughened to harden them for this purpose by digging them into a bowl of soft sand or rice. See Fig. 49.

There is usually only one attack made with these striking points.

(a) The Eyes

From the Open Leg Stance (Hachiji Dachi), step forward with

FIG 50

FIG 48

the V described. The hand still turns as you make the attack, being palm upward when it is on your hip and twisting to palm downward just before impact. The left hand also twists as it is withdrawn to the hip. See Fig. 48.

8. ATTACKS WITH THE FIRST TWO FINGERS SPREAD OPEN (NIHON NUKITE)

Spread the first two fingers wide apart. Bend the third and fourth

the right foot and make the attack with the right hand. The attack starts from the hip with the palm upward, and twists to palm downward just before impact. The left hand is brought back on to the left hip and twisted as usual. See Fig. 50.

9. ATTACKS WITH THE FIRST FINGER (IPPON NUKITE)

Keep the first finger straight. Bend the others so that they touch the top of the palm at their own bases. Bend the thumb into the palm, letting it lie where it does naturally, without forcing it farther in. The attacking point is

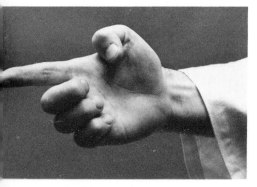

FIG 51

the end of the first finger. Again, it can be toughened by the exercises described for two fingers in the last section. It is obviously a very small attacking point suitable for penetrating small target areas. See Fig. 51.

We shall study two attacks with this.

(a) At the Eye

This needs no real explanation. Move in from the Open Leg Stance (Hachiji Dachi). As the right hand makes the attack, bring the left back on to the hip.

Be sure to shoot the attacking arm out straight as in all these blows. See Fig. 52.

(b) At the Solar Plexus

Take up the Forward Stance (Zenkutsu Dachi) facing the opponent, being close enough to deliver the attack with a reverse punch. The arm should be straight at the moment of impact,

FIG 52

twisting as usual, and the other hand brought back on to the hip. See Fig. 53.

10. ATTACKS WITH THE LITTLE FINGER EDGE OF THE HAND (SHUTO)

Try clenching your fist and then opening it to spread the fingers wide apart. If you do this you will notice that there is a muscle at

FIG 53

FIG 55

the bottom edge of the hand, which will stand out as you clench the hand. This muscle is the striking point. This particular blow is called a 'strike' because it is a 'chop' in common language, the arm and the hand being used rather like a chopper. See Fig. 54.

This area can be hardened by chopping on to a hard surface such as wood. The muscle itself can be developed, too, by holding the arms straight out in front at shoulder height and alternately opening and clenching the fists. We shall study three attacks made with this striking point.

(a) At the Ribs

From the Open Leg Stance (Hachiji Dachi), step forward with the left foot and then with the right, turning your right side to your opponent as you do so. Strike his right ribs, palm downward, taking the other hand back on to your left hip, palm upward. See Fig. 55.

The attack can also be made palm upward, of course.

(b) At the Throat

Move to your opponent's left side and on to the same line, turning to face the same way. Bend the right arm across your chest and swing it back from the elbow to make the chop against his Adam's apple, palm downward. As usual, bring the other hand back on to your left hip. See Fig. 56.

FIG 54

FIG 56

FIG 58

11. ATTACKS WITH THE FIRST THREE FINGERS (YONHON NUKITE)

Bend the first three fingers slightly so that the tips of them form a straight line. This, you will find, involves taking the second finger tip back a bit by bending it more than the first and third. Rest the thumb where it naturally lies on the palm, but without forcing it farther in. The attacking point is the combined tips of the three fingers, which form a kind of wedge. See Fig. 58.

We shall study two attacks with this.

(a) At the Lower Abdomen

From the Forward Stance (Zenkutsu Dachi), make a lunge

(c) At the Side of the Neck

Move to your opponent's right side by stepping forward with your left foot first, then right. With the side of your right hand, strike at the right side of his neck, bringing your left hand back on to your left hip. See Fig. 57.

FIG 57

FIG 59

punch with the right hand, attacking the lower abdomen. Twist the hand as you strike from palm upward to palm downward, and withdraw the other hand, twisting that also. To get the

12. ATTACKS WITH THE HEEL OF THE PALM (TEISHO)

Bend the fingers in to touch the top of the palm at the base of the fingers. Bend the thumb in to rest

FIG 60

FIG 62

greatest effect, drive the finger tips in and up. See Fig. 59.

(b) At the Testicles

Again, make the attack from the Forward Stance (Zenkutsu Dachi), Front Facing Posture. Use a lunge punch as in the last attack. See Fig. 60.

FIG 61

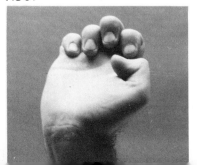

on the palm, but without forcing it farther in than it naturally lies. Bend the hand back at the wrist joint. The attacking point is the base of the palm where it joins the wrist. See Fig. 61.

We shall study two attacks with this.

(a) At the Base of the Nose

From the Open Leg Stance (Hachiji Dachi), simply step in, left foot first, then right and make the attack with the right hand, bringing the left back on to the hip in the usual way as you do so. Hit upward at an angle of forty-five degrees to your opponent's face. The object is to drive the bone of the nose back into the brain. See Fig. 62.

(b) At the Jaw

Make the attack exactly as described above, but this time hit under the chin. The object is to jerk the head back violently and dislocate the neck. See Fig. 63.

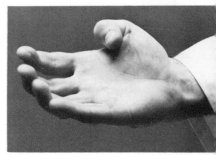

FIG 64

We shall study one attack with this.

(a) At the Collar-bone

From the Open Leg Stance (Hachiji Dachi), step forward with the right foot and bring the attacking point down sharply on the opponent's right collar-bone. Hit, not at it, but right through it, as if you were smashing a piece of wood. Bring the left hand back on to the left hip as you do so. The object is to shatter the bone. See Fig. 65.

FIG 65

FIG 63

13. ATTACKS WITH THE CURVE OF THE WRIST (SEIRYUTO)

Curl the fingers slightly inward, but do not bend them into the palm. Rest the thumb against its own side of the hand. Bend the hand back at the wrist joint. The attacking point is the edge of the wrist on the little finger side. It is used like a hammer. See Fig. 64.

14. ATTACKS WITH THE ELBOW (EMPI)

There is no need for a detailed description of this attacking point, nor illustration. It is simply the sharp point of your elbow, which is a most effective weapon when you bend your arm. We shall study three attacks with this.

elbow. From the Open Leg Stance (Hachiji Dachi), take the right foot forward, to bring you into a Side Facing Position and the Hour Glass Stance (Sanchin Dachi). Bring your right elbow up sideways to strike your opponent under the chin. The object is to jerk the head back and dislocate the neck. See Fig. 67.

Fig 66

(a) At the Ribs

Come to your opponent's left side, facing the same way, and take up the Open Leg Stance (Hachiji Dachi). Take your right arm across your chest and, keeping it bent, strike your opponent in his left ribs with the point of your right elbow. Bring your left fist back on to your left hip as you do so, twisting it to palm upward. See Fig. 66.

(b) At the Chin

This is an upward blow with the

Fig 67

(c) At the Kidneys

Step in with your left foot, then right, so that you come to the opponent's right side, slightly behind him. Bring your right elbow back sharply into his right kidney. As your right elbow is brought back, your left hand

FIG 68

shoots forward in this case, in a compensatory movement. See Fig. 68.

The above are only a selection of the possible attacks. Although they have all been described as right-hand attacks, you will realize that by reversing the directions they can be done as left-hand attacks. The starting positions and the movements in have only been given as examples of what is possible. In actual practice you can attack from whatever posture you happen to be in and from whatever position. Thus, if you are near, you will use reverse punches; if you are far away, you will use lunge punches to bring yourself in range. If you are upright and close, you will attack from the Open Leg Stance or the Hour Glass Stance; if your knees are bent, you will attack from the Straddle Leg Stance; if you are away, you will tend to attack from the Forward or the Backward Stances. You must first practise a few basic ones, such as we have described above, so that you can get accustomed to making an attack from a recognized stance, instead of rushing in wildly, which would lead to your being off balance, striking inaccurately and hence ineffectively. When you come to free practice, however, you must be inventive and look for any opportunity for any attack. The possibilities are endless.

Finally, let me repeat the warning previously given. In view of the very serious nature of any of these attacks, you must never land blows or strikes. You must stop just short of the target.

7. Kicks

Basically, there are three kinds of standing kick in karate: the snap kick, the thrust kick and the kick with the edge of the foot. The last named is rather like the chopping action with the edge of the hand.

Before going on to consider details of these, let us differentiate between a thrust kick and a snap kick. In each of them, the weight must be borne on the rear leg, with the heel on the ground and maintaining good balance. Do not lean backward as you kick or you will weaken your balance. Raise to your chest the knee of the foot you are going to kick with. The kicking foot must be at least as high off the ground as the knee of the leg on which you are standing.

THE SNAP KICK

From this position of knee up to chest, snap the kicking foot directly out at the target, from the knee joint, instantly returning it to the bent knee position, before lowering the leg. See Fig. 69.

THE THRUST KICK

The initial position is the same as for the snap kick. The knee is raised to the chest. This time, however, the foot is thrust out straight to the target, like a punch with the fist. Return it to the bent leg position before lowering the foot to the ground. See Fig. 70.

The object of bending the leg before lowering it to the ground

FIG 69

FIG 70

Fig 71

is to prevent your opponent from grabbing your foot or ankle and taking you off balance.

We shall now look at some of the striking points listed in Chapter 5 and give some examples of attacks with each.

Fig 72

Fig 73

1. ATTACKS WITH THE KNEE (HITTSUI)

There is no need to describe or illustrate this striking point. It is used for close-in attacks. We shall study three attacks with the knee.

(a) At the Face

From the Front Facing Posture, clasp your hands behind your opponent's head and bring his face down on to your knee, at the same time bringing your knee up to smash into his face. See Fig. 71.

(b) At the Solar Plexus

Again this can be done from a Front Facing Posture. You must be close to your opponent. Bring the knee up sharply and drive it in. See Fig. 72.

(c) At the Groin

Opportunity for this occurs if your opponent has his legs somewhat apart and is not quick enough to bring his knees together to save

himself. Catch his lapels with
both hands and pull him on to the
attack, which is at the testicles.
See Fig. 73.

2. ATTACKS WITH THE INSTEP (HAISOKU)

Raise your knee to your chest and
bend the toes downward. The
attacking point is the top of your
foot, midway between the base of
your toes and the ankle. See Fig.
74.

FIG 75

3. ATTACKS WITH THE FOOT EDGE (SOKUTO)

Raise your foot from the ground
and turn it outwards at the ankle
joint so that the edge of the foot
on the little toe side forms an
attacking point. See Fig. 76.

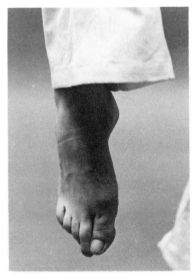

FIG 74

There is only one basic attack
with this.

(a) At the Groin

From the Front Facing Posture
and the Cat Stance (Neko Ashi
Dachi) Chapter 3, No. 5, bring the
knee up to the chest and use the
instep to make a snap kick at the
opponent's groin. See Fig. 75.

Be sure to bend the leg again
before you return the foot to the
ground.

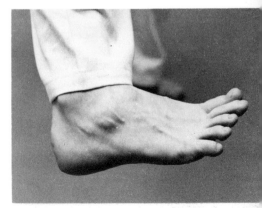

FIG 76

FIG 77

This is used in thrusting kicks. We shall study four examples.

(a) At the Knee

Take up the Cat Stance (Neko Ashi Dachi), with a Side Facing Posture. Let your left leg bear the weight, your right side be to your opponent and raise the right knee to the chest before making a thrust kick at his left knee-cap. See Fig. 77.

The object is to break the knee-cap. The attack is very powerful and will do serious damage, so practise with great care not to land the blow.

FIG 78

(b) At the Shin Bone

Do this from exactly the same stance and posture as the last movement, but this time let your target be your opponent's left shin bone. It will easily shatter the bone. See Fig. 78.

(c) At the Armpit

This is done when your opponent is striking you. For practice, let him strike at your face with his left fist. Side step to your left, turn to a Side Facing Posture and

FIG 79

with the left knee bent and supporting you make a side thrust kick with your right foot at his left armpit. The direction of the kick is upward. See Fig. 79.

(d) At the Lower Abdomen

Take up the Straddle Leg Stance (Kiba Dachi) in a Side Facing Posture with your right side towards the opponent. Attack with the edge of your right foot

FIG 80

FIG 81

with a sideways thrust kick. See Fig. 80.

4. ATTACKS WITH THE SOLE OF THE FOOT (TEISOKU)

The attacking point is the whole of the bottom of the foot. There is no need to illustrate. We shall look at one attack.

(a) At the Solar Plexus

From the Cat Stance (Neko Ashi Dachi), with the left foot to the rear and bearing the weight, raise the right foot. Face the opponent directly in the Front Facing Posture. From this position, make a thrust kick forward at his solar plexus. See Fig. 81.

5. ATTACKS WITH THE HEEL (KAKATO)

Again, there is no need to illustrate the attacking point. It is simply the area of the foot underneath the heel. We shall study three attacks with this.

(a) At the Jaw

Turn your back on your opponent. Bend forward, place both hands on the ground to support yourself and kick backward and upward with your heel at his jaw. See Fig. 82.

(b) At the Stomach

Turn your right side to your opponent. Drop your left hand to

FIG 82

FIG 83

high as possible, then bringing it down with all your force, transferring your weight on to it as you stamp down. Be careful not to lose your balance, however. See Fig. 84.

6. ATTACKS WITH THE BALL OF THE FOOT (KOSHI)

The attacking point is the front part of the bottom of the foot, just behind the toes. Bend the toes upwards when you use this attack. See Fig. 85.

the floor to support yourself and kick sideways with your right heel at his stomach. See Fig. 83.

(c) At the Instep

This is a stamping kick. From a Side Facing Posture stamp directly down on your opponent's instep, bending your knee first and lifting the attacking foot as

FIG 84

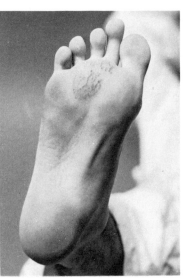

FIG 85

We shall study three attacks with this.

(a) At the Face

Take up the Cat Stance (Neko Ashi Dachi) with a Front Facing Posture, having your left leg to the rear, bearing the weight. Bring the right knee up to your chest and then make a thrust kick at your opponent's face. Avoid leaning backward as you do so because this would lessen the power of the kick and would put you off balance. Bring the foot back instantly to the bent position after the attack. See Fig. 86.

It makes it somewhat easier to do these high kicks if you bend the knee of the leg you are standing on and straighten it to give yourself the extra height as you attack.

(b) At the Solar Plexus

From the same stance and

FIG 87

There are also leaping or flying kicks when you jump up in the air to deliver the kick, but these are rather advanced movements and not suitable for a basic book such as this.

As in the case of blows or strikes with the hands, the examples given in this chapter are only a few of the possible attacks. Practise these first, but then go on to invent your own.

Remember, too, that they are all highly dangerous. Never land any one of them. Stop just short of the target.

FIG 88

FIG 86

posture as the last movement, make a thrust kick at your opponent's solar plexus. See Fig. 87.

(c) At the Ribs

Take up the Cat Stance (Neko Ashi Dachi) with your weight on your left foot and somewhat to your opponent's right side. Raise the right knee and make a thrusting kick sideways at his right ribs. See Fig. 88.

All the above are standing kicks because you are standing firm on the ground when you make them.

8. Blocks

Karate should not be used for aggressive purposes; indeed the only justification for its use outside of practice would be self-defence in dire emergency. Even then, as little damage should be done as possible. From the ethical point of view, judo is a much better form of self-defence because it enables you to overcome your opponent without hurting him.

The blocks in karate are very important because they enable you not only to ward off attacks, but are in themselves so painful that they might discourage the opponent from attacking again. We shall study seven blocks made with either hand or arm and two made with the leg and give an example of the use of each of them.

1. THE DOWNWARD BLOCK (GEDAN BARAI)

Stand upright with the left fist held forward, arm straight in

FIG 89

FIG 90

FIG 91

front of you, knuckles upward
and the right fist on your right
hip, knuckles downward. See Fig.
89.

From this position, take the right
fist across your chest and up to
your left ear. Now, to make the
downward block with your right
arm, you bring the right fist down
across your chest, straightening
the arm so as to deflect an
imaginary blow or kick aimed at
the lower part of your body. As
your right arm descends to make
this block, your left must
simultaneously be withdrawn on
to your left hip, turning the
knuckles downward as you do so.
See Fig. 90.
   This withdrawal at the same
time is essential to increase the
force of the block and to bring the
fist in position for the
counter-attack that will normally
follow the block. Do not swing
the blocking arm too far from
your body. It should not go
beyond your side to the right.
   As an example, stand in the
Forward Stance (Zenkutsu Dachi)
and let your opponent take up the
same stance facing you with his
right foot forward and far enough
away to make a lunge punch with
his left at your solar plexus,

FIG 92

bringing his left foot forward as
he does so, of course. Block this
with a downward block, using
your right arm. See Fig. 91.

It will be seen that this block can
be used against any blow or kick
aimed at the lower parts of the
body, such as the lower
abdomen, the testicles, the solar
plexus, etc.

2. THE UPWARD BLOCK (AGE UKE)
Stand upright, fists clenched and
held in front of you, in the Open
Leg Stance (Hachiji Dachi). To
make the upward block, take the
right fist across the front of your
body, turning and raising the
forearm to deflect an attacking
arm upward. At the top of your
movement, your right forearm
should be level with your
forehead and the fist twisted so
that the back of the hand is
towards your face and the palm

side outward. As you are making this block with your right arm, you withdraw the left to the left hip, twisting it to palm upward. This adds force to the block and prepares you to counter-attack. See Fig. 92.

To practise, block first with your right arm withdrawing the left, and then with the left withdrawing the right, alternately, concentrating first on accuracy of movement and then on increasing speed. Be careful not to take your elbow too far from your body, nor to raise your elbow higher than the blocking arm, because either mistake will weaken your block. At the moment of blocking, the forearm should not be more than about three inches from your face.

As an example, take up the Open Leg Stance (Hachiji Dachi).

Fig 93

Let your opponent do the same and let him attack your chin with a simple right-handed punch. Block it with a right-handed block and move back into a Forward Stance (Zenkutsu Dachi) by taking your left leg back, as you block. See Fig. 93.

This block can be used against an attack made at the face, throat or upper chest area.

3. THE INSIDE BLOCK (UDE UKE)

Stand upright, fists clenched, in the Open Leg Stance (Hachiji Dachi). Raise the right arm, bending it at ninety degrees at the elbow so that the fist is level with your shoulder. Take the elbow across your body so that your right fist is opposite your left shoulder. See Fig. 94.

Now, from this position, move your right forearm across your own body to deflect a blow to your own right. While you are moving the right fist in this way, bring the left on to your left hip, twisting it to knuckles downward. See Fig. 95.

Your right elbow must not go beyond the right side of your body when making the block. This is called an inside block because it blocks the inside of an attacking arm.

As an example, take up the Open Leg Stance (Hachiji Dachi). Let your opponent make a lunge punch with his left hand at your chin. Block with the right-handed inside block, at the same time taking your left foot back into the Forward Stance (Zenkutsu Dachi). See Fig. 96.

This block can be used against any attack on the upper part of the body or the head.

FIG 94

FIG 95

4. THE OUTSIDE BLOCK (UDE UKE)

This block has the same Japanese name because it is exactly the same movement on your part. The only difference is that this time, you deflect your opponent's arm by striking it on the outside instead of the inside.

In the example of the movement used as an inside block, which we have just studied, the opponent attacked your chin with his left. Consider the same situation when he attacks with his right. You make exactly the same blocking movement, but this time, instead of the block connecting with the inside of his left arm, it connects with the outside of his right. See Fig. 97.

FIG 96

FIG 97

FIG 98

This block can be used in any of the situations where an inside block could be used. It will be seen from the illustrations that if you block with the same arm as he attacks with, you will normally do an outside block; if you block with the opposite arm to that with which he attacks you (i.e. your right against his left), you will get an inside block.

5. THE KNIFE HAND BLOCK (SHUTO UKE)

So far, we have been considering blocks made with the fists clenched. This is the safest way for a beginner to practise because it tenses the forearm muscles and the clenched fist prevents injury to the fingers. The knife hand block, however, is made with the fingers open, and is often combined with the strike with the side of the hand (Shuto), described in Chapter 6, No. 10. If the strike is on the elbow joint of an opponent's attacking arm, it could cause dislocation. The knife hand block can be an upward, downward, inside or outside

block. Practise all the ones you have learnt as knife hand blocks, that is with the hands open. We illustrate it as a downward knife hand block. See Fig. 98.

As an example, stand in the normal Open Leg Stance (Hachiji Dachi). Let your opponent attack with a right-handed lunge punch to your body. Step back into the

FIG 99

FIG 100

your body by bringing your left fist close to it and pushing on the elbow. See Fig. 100.

As an example, take up the Back Stance (Kokutsu Dachi) and let your opponent make a right-handed reverse punch at the upper part of your body. Block it with the outside augmented forearm block, as shown in Fig. 101.

This block can be used against any attack for which the inside or outside block would be appropriate and gives extra blocking power against a very powerful attack.

7. THE CROSS BLOCK (JUJI UKE)

This block is made by crossing the arms in front of you just below the wrists. Keep the hands open, ready to grab the opponent, unless you are

Back Stance (Kokutsu Dachi) by taking the left leg back, at the same time making the downward knife hand block with your right hand against his right elbow joint. You will note that you are turning your body into a half Front Facing Posture as you do so. See Fig. 99.

This block can be used against any of the attacks previously mentioned.

6. THE AUGMENTED FOREARM BLOCK (MOROTE UKE)

This is similar to the inside or outside blocks (Ude Uke) except that the opposite hand is used to augment the block instead of being taken back on to the hip. Practise making the inside block, as described in No. 3 of this chapter, but from the position shown in Figure 94 assist the taking of your right elbow across

FIG 101

blocking a kick, in which case close the fists to avoid injury to the fingers. Keep the elbows close to your body, letting them brush your hips as your arms shoot straight out to make this block. The block can be made either upward, against high attacks, or downward, against low attacks. From the Straddle Leg Stance (Kiba Dachi), thrust both hands forward and upward so that they cross at a point level with the top of your forehead. If you are right-handed, keep your right arm nearer your body and your left on the outside nearer your opponent. See Fig. 102.

FIG 103

As an example, we will look at the block used downward. Stand in the Straddle Leg Stance (Kiba Dachi). Your opponent faces you in a Forward Stance (Zenkutsu Dachi). He kicks you in the groin with his right foot. As he does so, block with the downward cross block. See Fig. 103.

This block is very useful because it can be used against either high or low attacks and against attacks with arms or feet.

8. THE INSIDE BLOCK WITH THE LEG (NAMI ASHI)

This is one of the two blocks with the legs and feet. Take up the Straddle Leg Stance (Kiba Dachi). Raise the right foot off the ground, bending the leg at the knee so that the foot is brought almost level with the body. Then snap it down again to its original position, using the force of so doing to deflect an attacking foot or fist. See Fig. 104.

FIG 102

FIG 104

FIG 105

As an example, stand in the Straddle Leg Stance (Kiba Dachi). Let your opponent aim a left-footed kick at your groin. Block with an inside block with the leg, as described above. See Fig. 105.

This block can be used against any attack that is low down, even those that are made with the fist. In this case you may need to raise the blocking leg a little higher to get it over his arm.

9. THE OUTSIDE BLOCK WITH THE LEG (NAMI ASHI)

This has the same Japanese name because in essence it is the same movement. As with the same two blocks made with the arms, if you block by pushing on the inside of an attacking leg you are doing an inside block, and if you push on the outside you are doing an outside block.

As an example, let us look at its use against a low punch with the fist. Stand in the Straddle Leg Stance (Kiba Dachi). From the Forward Stance let the opponent make a lunge punch at your groin with his right hand. Block with the outside block with the leg as shown in the illustration. See Fig. 106.

FIG 106

This block has exactly the same uses as the previous one.

Practise all these blocks, both on your own and with a partner attacking you. A good way of doing the latter is for you both to take up the Forward Stance (Zenkutsu Dachi) facing each other, at one end of the room. Now, let him advance, making lunge punches with alternate hands on each step he takes, while you retreat in time with him, making the appropriate blocks. The methods of advance and retreat are detailed in Chapter 4.

Choose in advance which attack and which block you are going to practise. As an example, he could make lunge punches at your face and you could

block with the upward block.

When you reach the end of the room, come back with you attacking and your partner blocking. This gives you both practice. Karate experts will spend hours in this kind of training, making the movements slowly at first to get both the attacks and the blocks smooth and accurate. Then they will aim for more speed.

When you are experienced at this, try doing the same exercise with varied attacks, and then without pre-arranging which attack is going to be made so that you get used to meeting instantly the situation that arises. Space yourselves at the right distance before you begin so that no blow is actually landed.

9. Kumites

So far, we have learnt simple attacks and simple means of blocking those attacks. The next stage is to learn counter-attacks to follow on after we have blocked. Obviously there are thousands of such combinations of attack, block, and counter-attack. These combinations are called 'kumites'. They are practised as entirely pre-arranged sequences of movement. The attack, the block and the counter-attack are all decided upon. The one partner makes the attack and the other blocks and counters. Then they reverse their roles so that each gets practice.

Before attempting this form of practice, you must both have developed sufficient skill to be able to stop just short of landing any blow or kick.

As examples of what is possible, we will consider some of the attacks described in Chapters 6 and 7 and for each of the attacks, learn a block and counter. It must be emphasized, however, that these are only examples of what is possible. Other blocks and counters could be used for any one of the attacks. You must invent your own to practise as well and go on inventing and practising as many combinations as you can. The unusual ones that you can think out for yourself will have the advantage of catching your opponent by surprise in a contest, whereas the common ones are well known and expected.

Again, the warning must be repeated; never land a blow or kick, either in attack or counter-attack.

Many of the counters involve shifting your position as you block, so that you will be in a position to counter-attack effectively. Study again the information on how to move given in Chapter 4. The ideal in karate is to do as little as possible. Try to end the conflict with one movement, be it attack, block, or counter-attack. Make each movement serious and in earnest, as though you had only that one chance to stop the other man and your life depended on doing so. Focus each punch as described in Chapter 1.

1. BLOCK AND COUNTER TO TWO-KNUCKLE ATTACK ON BRIDGE OF NOSE

The opponent makes the attack described in Chapter 6, No. 1(a). Block with the upward block (Age Uke), then open the left hand so that you can grasp the opponent's sleeve when you have blocked. See Fig. 107.

Having blocked, step forward with your right foot and pull the opponent on to an elbow strike to his jaw. See Fig. 108.

Fig 107

Fig 108

2. BLOCK AND COUNTER TO BACK-FIST ATTACK AT SOLAR PLEXUS

The opponent makes the attack described in Chapter 6, No. 2(b). Turn by moving away from the attack and block with the inside block (Ude Uke) with your left hand. See Fig. 109.

Catch his arm and pull him on to a snap kick to his ribs with your right foot. See Fig. 110.

3. BLOCK AND COUNTER TO BOTTOM-FIST ATTACK ON CLAVICLE

The opponent makes the attack described in Chapter 6, No. 3(b). Block with a rising grasping block (Shuto Uke) with your left hand. See Fig. 111.

Fig 109

Fig 110

FIG 111

FIG 112

Counter by making an attack on his ribs with your right elbow, turning your left side away from him and pulling him on to the attack. See Fig. 112.

Block with a left-handed inside block (Ude Uke). See Fig. 113.

4. BLOCK AND COUNTER TO ONE-FINGER ATTACK ON SOLAR PLEXUS

The opponent makes the attack described in Chapter 6, No. 9(b).

Counter with a kick at his right knee with your right foot. See Fig. 114.

5. BLOCK AND COUNTER TO EDGE-OF-HAND ATTACK AT RIBS

The opponent makes the attack

FIG 113

FIG 114

FIG 115

FIG 116

described in Chapter 6, No. 10(a).
Block with the right-handed
downward block (Gedan Barai).
See Fig. 115.

Counter with a right-footed kick at
his testicles. See Fig. 116.

6. BLOCK AND COUNTER TO THREE-FINGER ATTACK AT LOWER ABDOMEN

Your opponent makes the attack
described in Chapter 6, No. 11(a).
Block with a left-handed

FIG 117

FIG 118

FIG 119

downward block (Gedan Barai).
See Fig. 117.

Counter with a kick to his right
shin with the edge of your right
foot. See Fig. 118.

7. BLOCK AND COUNTER TO PALM-HEEL ATTACK ON JAW

Your opponent makes the attack
described in Chapter 6, No. 12(b).

FIG 120

Block with a left-handed upward
block (Age Uke). See Fig. 119.

Counter by striking the top of his
skull with the bottom of your fist.
See Fig. 120.

8. BLOCK AND COUNTER TO ELBOW ATTACK AT RIBS

Your opponent makes the attack
described in Chapter 6, No. 14(a).

FIG 121

FIG 122

FIG 123

FIG 124

Turn towards him to avoid the attack. See Fig. 121.

Counter by kicking his rear knee with the edge of your right foot and striking his right temple with the back of your right fist. See Fig. 122.

9. BLOCK AND COUNTER TO KNEE ATTACK AT FACE

Your opponent makes the attack described in Chapter 7, No. 1(a).

Step to your right and in your left hand catch the knee he is bringing up. See Fig. 123.

Counter by bringing your right knee up into his testicles. See Fig. 124.

10. BLOCK AND COUNTER TO ATTACK AT GROIN WITH INSTEP

Your opponent makes the attack described in Chapter 7, No. 2(a). Block with an inside block with

FIG 125

FIG 126

FIG 127

FIG 128

your left leg (Nami Ashi). See Fig. 125.

Counter with a right-handed punch to his jaw using the first two knuckles of the hand. See Fig. 126.

11. BLOCK AND COUNTER TO ATTACK AT KNEE WITH FOOT EDGE

Your opponent makes the attack described in Chapter 7, No. 3(a). Do the outside block with your left leg (Nami Ashi). See Fig. 127.

You will find that this turns his back to you enough to enable you to attack the base of his skull with the back of your right fist. See Fig. 128.

FIG 129

FIG 130

12. BLOCK AND COUNTER TO ATTACK AT SOLAR PLEXUS WITH SOLE OF FOOT

Your opponent makes the attack described in Chapter 7, No. 4(a). Catch the attacking foot with both hands and lift it, to unbalance him. Step back out of range as you do this. See Fig. 129.

Counter with a right thrust kick to his testicles. See Fig. 130.

The above suggestions give you the idea of kumites. Go on and invent more for yourself. Remember, however, that it is better to master one or two than just to know a hundred. The one that you can bring off is worth the ninety and nine that are just not quite good enough for success.

10. Semi-free and Free Practice and Contest

The karate student begins by practising the basic moves by himself, without a partner, to obtain smoothness and proficiency of movement and to develop self-control. He then goes on to practise moves and counter-moves in pre-arranged forms from a standing position with a partner. The kumites dealt with in the last chapter are examples of these. The next stage in his study is semi-free practice.

SEMI-FREE PRACTICE

In this, the form of attack, the target and the block and counter to be practised are all pre-arranged, as in the kumites, but instead of doing them from a static position the partners move around and the attacker must try to find a suitable opening for the attack. Both must be relaxed and move freely, but not rush around aimlessly. In general, the less movement the better, because movement not only uses up energy, but is liable to put you off balance. Remember strong attacks and strong blocks can only be made from strong stances.

When you have made some progress with this form of semi-free practice, there is a more advanced variation. That is to pre-determine who is to attack and who is to defend, but not to arrange which attacks or defences are to be used. One man attacks, the other defends, but the attacks are those that arise naturally from the exploitation of momentary weaknesses and the defences are the instinctive reactions to those attacks. In this form of practice the defender never initiates attack, so that the attacker can move in freely, knowing that he has only to exploit openings in his partner's defence and does not also have to watch for attacks on himself. It is thus a half-way stage to full free practice. The partners change their roles at intervals and the defender becomes the attacker in turn.

FREE PRACTICE

This is the next step forward from semi-free practice. Free practice corresponds to sparring in boxing or to randori in judo. Nothing is pre-arranged. The partners bow to each other and then move around, trying whatever attacks, blocks, counter-attacks, continuous attacks, etc., that offer opportunities.

If it is to be of value, it must be practised with self-discipline. You must consciously look for openings, focus your punches correctly, aim at the precise targets, hit correctly, move correctly and remember all the time the need for accuracy. If you just rush wildly about, striking and kicking in the hope that something will connect, it is not only useless it is positively dangerous.

Blows and kicks must never be landed. As in all forms of practice, they must stop just short of the target. But while bearing this in mind, you must picture your opponent as a real enemy and practise as seriously as if you were fighting for your life. With each blow, think that it is the only move left to win. Ideally, in a real fight, a karate expert would aim at disabling his opponent with one movement and one movement only. Particularly if you should ever be attacked in earnest by several assailants, this ability to dispose of each of them with just one movement would give you a chance of winning. So remember that it is this for which you are constantly aiming— speed, accuracy, power.

You must not only look out for openings that occur as the result of your opponent's movements or relaxing of his guard, but you must try to create such openings by feinting as in boxing. As well as blocking attacks with the blocks you have learnt, you must get used to avoiding others simply by moving out of the way.

At the end of practice, partners bow to each other, as they did in the beginning because courtesy to one's partner is one of the important aspects of the sport. Friendship and mutual respect should be the ruling spirit of your meeting. You are there to improve each other, and anyone who gives up his time to helping you improve is worthy of your respect, whatever his ability in relation to your own.

Free practice is not for beginners. You must advance through the other stages first. It is tempting to go on to it in the early stages because it looks more exciting than just repeating basic movements, but if you start too soon you will impede your own progress as a whole because you will not have the skill that makes free practice valuable, and under the stresses of moving about, you will allow errors of style and inaccuracy of focusing to creep in. Once these errors become ingrained in your style, you will find them very difficult to eradicate.

CONTEST

Contests have been organized in karate only since 1957, when a Japanese University match took place. Although in Western countries, students below the stage of Black Belt are allowed to participate in inter-club events, it should be borne in mind that contests are not for beginners. Ideally, they should be only for Black Belts.

The first thing to remember is that blows and kicks must never be landed. If you do land a blow or kick, it is a foul and you will lose.

Contests take place in an area approximately 7·5 m (24 ft) square. The edges of the square should be clearly marked and there should be a clear space of at least 30 cm (1 ft) around this.

There is a referee, who controls the contest and who is able to move around the square with the contestants. There are also four judges, who are stationed at the four corners. Each is provided with a whistle, a red flag and a white flag. When they want to call the referee's attention to something, they blow the whistle. When the referee asks them to indicate their decision, they do so by raising the appropriate flag or the crossed flags for a draw. As in boxing, one of the contestants wears a small red slip tied to his belt and is spoken of as being 'in the red corner'. The other is in the white corner. Judges hold the red flag in the right hand and the white one in the left.

In addition to the referee and judges, there is a timekeeper. He indicates the time the contest should terminate, calculating from the referee's command to begin and allowing for any time out that has been sanctioned. The usual length of a contest is two minutes. Sometimes three-minute contests are held. Sometimes extra time will be allowed. It will be seen, therefore, that swift decisive action is needed for success.

Above the officials already named, there is the controller. He is in charge of the day's proceedings and will generally be a very experienced master. If he sees anything wrong, he can call the attention of the referee or judges to it. If a contestant disagrees with a decision, he can ask his team manager to approach the controller, who could ask the referee to reconsider his verdict. Apart from this, the referee's decision is final. Contestants never approach a judge or the referee or the controller themselves. It must always be done through their team manager.

At the beginning of any meeting, the referee and the four judges line up at one side of the area and all the contestants line up at the other. Together they make the kneeling bow to each other. Following this, the contestants sit down until called and the referee and judges go to their appointed places.

When two contestants are called forward, they stand at a distance of 180 cm (6 ft), with the referee to one side and midway between them. They all make the standing bow together. The referee then calls 'Hajime', which means 'Begin'. Unless there is time out for injury or for consultation with the judges, the contest lasts for two minutes from this command. A bell is rung after one and a half minutes to indicate that only half a minute is left. A second bell is rung at 'time'. The referee then calls 'Soremade', which means 'That is all'. He then announces his decision, if necessary consulting with the judges first. The contestants and referee then all make the standing bow as in the beginning.

If the contestants go outside the area, the referee will stop them and bring them back. If a point is scored, the referee will call 'Ippon' and the contest is over. If a half-point is scored, the referee will call 'Waza-Ari'. If no points have been scored at the end, the referee asks the judges to indicate their decision by raising their flags. He is not bound by a majority verdict, however, but gives his own. In the event of a foul, the referee stops the contest and announces 'Hansoku Make', which means 'Lost by foul'. If the referee did not see it, a judge could call his attention to the act.

A point (Ippon) is awarded for a correctly focused punch that landed effectively on the target. This can be either an attack or a counter-attack. A half-point

(Waza-Ari) is awarded for a well-timed punch that is slightly off target, or a weak punch that is none the less well directed and finds the opponent off guard. If there is no score, the points looked for in reaching a decision are: skilful technique, good movement, fighting spirit, correct attitude to opponent and officials. By 'fighting spirit' an attacking style is meant. A defensive competitor has less chance than one who attacks.

The following actions are banned and constitute fouls:

1. Actually landing any blow or kick.
2. Attacking the opponent's eyes with a thrust, either with one finger, two fingers, or the second knuckles. The attack must not even be attempted, let alone landed.
3. Biting or clawing.
4. Holding in a clinch, as in boxing.
5. Stalling to waste time.
6. Showing disrespect to the opponent, or trying to make him lose his temper.

If either of the contestants does lose his temper, or if both become so excited that they lose control, then the referee will stop the contest, call them to the centre of the area and warn them, before allowing it to continue.

Any act of disrespect either to the opponent or to any official leads to immediate disqualification. It should be said, however, that such behaviour would be unthinkable to a properly trained karate man.

At the end of the meeting, the judges and referee again line up at one side of the area and the contestants at the other. Together they make the kneeling bow as a sign of respect and friendship. As they met, so they part friends.

Apart from tournaments, contests form part of grading examinations in the higher grades. Although they are sometimes used in the lower grades to see how much a student remembers under stress, they are not given as much importance as general knowledge, style and attitude.

11. Karate Applied to Self-defence

The student who has become proficient at the earlier movements in this book will not normally need to fear an ordinary assailant. Even the self-confidence induced by his skill may show in his manner sufficiently to deter anyone from attacking him. In any event, he has the knowledge to disable with one movement only.

One of the factors determining success in a fight is self-confidence. Do not be flustered or angry because excitement or anger produces tension and tension inhibits the free movement that will bring success. Think in terms of winning quickly, just as you must do in a karate contest. Fights should never be protracted and as little injury should be done to the opponent as is possible, consistent with the circumstances and the necessity of preventing further attack.

In this chapter, we shall look at a few practical situations and see how karate can be used to overcome a real-life assailant. The examples given will enable you to invent further applications of your own.

1. DEFENCE AGAINST SEIZURE AROUND THE ARMS FROM BEHIND

The attacker grabs you around the arms from behind. Before he can tighten his grip, spread your arms. See Fig. 131.

Move your body to your left. Bring your right elbow back into

Fig 131

Fig 132

FIG 133

FIG 134

his solar plexus, and stamp on his left instep with your right heel. See Fig. 132.

2. DEFENCE AGAINST A BUTT IN THE FACE

The assailant comes up to you, grabs your left lapel with his right hand and attempts to pull you forward into a butt in the face. Raise your right arm, elbow bent,

and jab your elbow into his throat. See Fig. 133.

This pushes him away from you and the pain in his throat disconcerts him. Move closer to his right side and behind him, so that you can jab your elbow into his kidney. See Fig. 134.

3. DEFENCE AGAINST A HOLD ON THE SLEEVE

Approaching from behind, the assailant grabs your left sleeve with his right hand. Instantly turn to face him and with your right hand, drive the heel of your palm up under his chin. This bends him

FIG 135

FIG 136

FIG 138

FIG 137

backwards, so that by putting your right foot behind his, as shown in Fig. 135, you can throw him backwards over it. See Fig. 135.

When he is down, drop on your right knee on his breastbone and deliver a right-handed two-knuckle punch to his face. See Fig. 136.

4. DEFENCE AGAINST A KNEE ATTACK TO THE GROIN

Coming close and grabbing your lapels in his hands, the assailant tries to bring his right knee up into your groin. Step quickly to your left and catch the knee in your right hand, so taking it to your right. You will now easily unbalance him in a backward direction. See Fig. 137.

Put your right foot behind his other leg and you can push him

back over it by lifting the knee you are holding and pulling down on his right sleeve with your left hand. As he falls, come down on him, right knee in his solar plexus and right hand jabbing at his Adam's apple, using the second knuckles. See Fig. 138.

5. DEFENCE AGAINST A KNIFE ATTACK TO THE STOMACH

The oft-pictured knife stab downward is, in fact, rarely used. Knife attacks are normally made as thrusts to the ribs, or heart, or stomach. Basically, the same defence is adaptable to all these. The assailant stabs directly forward at your stomach. Turn your body to face side-on to the direction of his thrust, and the thrust will then go past you. Catch the attacking wrist in your right hand, so that he cannot withdraw it for a second attempt, and chop at the side of his neck with the little finger edge of your left hand. See Fig. 139.

If further action is needed, bring

FIG 139

FIG 140

his elbow back against your stomach, thrusting the stomach forward so as to put painful pressure on his elbow and lead him to drop the knife. Hold his right shoulder down with your left hand while doing this. See Fig. 140.

6. DEFENCE AGAINST A COSH ATTACK TO YOUR HEAD

The assailant tries to strike you on top of the skull with a cosh.

This is usually done with a view to knocking you out, but if it is a heavy cosh it can fracture your skull, so the attack puts you in serious danger.

Step in, making the upward block (Age Uke) with your left hand. Thrust under his chin with the heel of your right palm. If you catch his wrist (holding the cosh) with your left hand, after blocking, and force it still farther back, you can throw him backward by the combined push on his wrist and thrust under his chin. See Fig. 141.

When he goes down, use your right knee to jab him in the

FIG 141

FIG 142

testicles, and punch him between the eyes with the one-knuckle punch delivered with the right hand. See Fig. 142.

7. DEFENCE AGAINST AN ASSAILANT WHO HAS KNOCKED YOU DOWN

You have been knocked down backward. Instantly put your right foot behind the assailant's right heel, with the instep pressing against his heel from the outside, and with your left foot make a thrusting kick at either his shin-bone or his knee-cap. It would shatter the shin-bone, or severely damage the knee-cap, and will put him down and out of action. See Fig. 143.

Fig 143

Fig 144

Fig 145

8. DEFENCE AGAINST TWO ASSAILANTS

Two men grab you, each holding an arm. This is often done so that a third may approach to hit you. Yield to the pull of the one who is stronger. This brings you close to him and gives you room to make a thrusting side kick with the edge of your foot against the knee-cap of the other. See Fig. 144.

This will put the one down. Turn and attack the other with the palm of your right hand, using the thrust with the heel of the palm to dislocate his neck. See Fig. 145.

As in all branches of karate, self-defence depends on practising each movement until it becomes instinctive. Success can only be attained with the aid of a partner who is prepared to repeat the movements hundreds of times with you until you are both performing them correctly. You must then speed them up with still more repetitions. Remember, you do not have time to think what to do if you are attacked in earnest. You must react with the instinctive response that only this kind of practice can give you.

12. Kata

A 'kata' is a ritual performance of a sequence of movements, performed on your own, so that the sequence forms a complete whole. It visualizes a number of imaginary opponents who are attacking you successively causing you to turn, block and counter-attack first one and then another in a pre-arranged sequence. Your skill at doing this is a measure of your progress and kata forms part of a grading test in karate.

As in judo katas, absolute accuracy must be sought when performing a kata. Thus, every turn must be made accurately, every block effectively, every blow must be a focused blow aimed at a specific target on the imaginary opponent. To achieve a high standard of performance you must practise katas hundreds of times. Aim at accuracy first and do not worry about speed. Only when you have gained a high degree of accuracy should you think of speeding up. It is generally considered that it takes three years to learn one kata. There are about thirty of them. In this chapter we shall study a simple one that is usually taught to beginners.

It is based on the pattern of a letter H. Imagine this H as a big letter chalked out on the floor and you will be able to carry out the movements correctly.

There are twenty-two movements and the techniques you need to know are the downward block (Gedan Barai) and the lunge punch (Oi Zuki), with basic movement and turns.

To begin, stand just one pace from the letter H at the point where the cross-piece joins the upright facing across to the other upright. Make the formal standing bow, heels together, as in Fig. 2. Then step forward to open your feet to normal distance. The twenty-two moves are then as follows:

1. Take up the basic Open Leg Stance (Hachiji Dachi) with fists clenched correctly and held in front of you.
2. Take your left fist to your right ear and make a turn to your left, moving into the Forward Stance (Zenkutsu Dachi) and making a downward block (Gedan Barai) against an imaginary opponent coming at you from the top of the upright of the H. As you are making the block, your right fist comes back on to your right hip, knuckles down, ready for attack.
3. Make a right-handed lunge punch to the solar plexus of this imaginary opponent, bringing your right foot forward as you do so, of course, and your left fist back on to your left hip.
4. Your next opponent is now behind you, coming from the other end of the upright of the H, so you must make a reverse turn by swivelling on your left foot to take up the Forward Stance

(Zenkutsu Dachi) facing the opposite way. As you turn, you must make the downward block (Gedan Barai) against his attack. To do this, take your right fist to your left ear and bring it down to block as you are turning.

5. You now attack this opponent with a left-handed lunge punch at his solar plexus, moving your left foot forward and bringing your right fist back on to your right hip.

6. Your next opponent is coming down the cross-piece of the H, so you make a quarter-turn to face him, swinging your left foot round and swivelling on your right. As you turn you make the downward block (Gedan Barai) with your left hand. Take it to your right ear and bring it down in the block as usual. At the position of blocking it should not be more than the width of two fists from your thigh. Your right fist will already be on your right hip ready for attack.

7. You now make three lunge punches in succession down the cross-piece of the H, moving forward correctly as you do so and bringing the opposite fist back on to the hip each time. The first punch is with the right.

8. Then a lunge punch with your left. All the targets are the same—his solar plexus.

9. Next a lunge punch with your right again. This brings you to the other upright of your H.

10. Your next opponent is coming up the upright of your H from your right-hand side. You must make a three-quarter turn, swivelling on your right foot, which is to the front, and bringing your left around. At the same time, you take your left fist to your right ear and bring it down with the downward block (Gedan

Barai) against his attack at your solar plexus. Your right fist comes back on to your right hip as you do so.

11. You now attack this opponent with a right-handed lunge punch at his solar plexus, bringing your left fist back on to your left hip and, of course, advancing your right foot. The attack is directly down the upright of the H.

12. Your next.opponent is directly behind you, coming from the opposite end of the upright of the H. You must, therefore, do an about-turn by taking the right foot to your right and around, swivelling on your left. As you do so, take the right fist to the left ear and bring it down in the downward block (Gedan Barai). Your left fist stays where it is on your hip ready for attack.

13. Make a left-handed lunge punch at his solar plexus, advancing your left foot as you do so and bringing your right fist back on to your right hip.

14. Your next opponent is coming up the cross-piece of the H, so you must make a quarter-turn to your left by swivelling on your right foot and bringing your left round. As you do so, take your left fist to your right ear and make the downward block (Gedan Barai) with your left hand. Your right fist remains on your right hip ready for attack.

15. You now make three lunge punches down the cross-piece of the H, beginning with the right fist.

16. Then the left.

17. Then the right again, which brings you to the other upright of the H.

18. Your next opponent is coming down the upright of the H from your right, so you must make a three-quarter about-turn to your

right by swivelling on your right foot, which is in front, and taking your left round to face him. As you do so, make the downward block (Gedan Barai) with your left hand by taking it to your right ear and bringing it down in the block. At the same time, bring your right fist back on to your right hip ready for attack.

19. Attack this opponent with the usual lunge punch with your right fist, stepping forward with your right foot and bringing your left fist back on to your left hip.

20. Your next opponent is coming from directly behind you, up the upright of the H. You make a reverse turn by swivelling on your left foot, which is to the rear, and bringing your right round to face him. At the same time, do the downward block (Gedan Barai) by taking your right fist to your left ear and bringing it down as you turn. Your left fist is already on your left hip ready for attack.

21. Attack this opponent with a lunge punch with your left, bringing your left foot forward and your right fist back on to your right hip.

22. This being the end of the set, you turn to face along the cross-piece of the H, bringing both fists to the ready position in front of you as you do so and taking up the Open Leg Stance (Hachiji Dachi) from which you started.

Step back one pace to bring your heels together and end the kata as you began it, with the formal standing bow.

13. Karate Exercises

In Chapter 2 we studied simple warming-up exercises. In this chapter we shall learn some more exercises which are specifically designed for karate training.

1. THE MAKIWARA BOARD

This is a board on which to practise your punches. Constant use of it will toughen your hands. There are two varieties. The first is a board about 140 cm (4½ ft) in height, which has the bottom anchored in the ground and the top flexible enough to give a little when hit. Around this board some padding is fastened, usually either straw or felt. It is then used for practising the lunge punch and the reverse punch.

The second form is a small hard board, also padded, which one partner holds in his hands while the other practises punches against it. This form has the advantage that it can be held in front of any selected target on the body and gives opportunity for a greater variety of punches and strikes.

Both boards can be used for punches with the fist, strikes with the edge of the hand, or any of the other blows or kicks described.

2. THE PUNCH BALL

Basically this is a leather ball, tethered by stout elastic from floor to ceiling, and it is used to practise hitting a moving target.

Move about as you try to punch with each hand in turn.

3. THE PUNCH BAG

This is a heavy bag, filled with a mixture of sand and sawdust, suspended from the ceiling. It gives opportunity to train at punching hard, or at kicking.

4. As has been mentioned earlier in this book, the fingers can be strengthened by stabbing them into a bucket of fine sand or rice.

Another good exercise is to hold the hands out at shoulder-level in front of you and to alternately clench the fists, then spread the fingers wide. Fifty repetitions of this will leave the wrists aching and convince you of its efficacy.

5. To strengthen the legs, take up a position with one knee almost on the ground and the other bent. The rear one is the one nearly touching the ground. Now, move forward by taking the rear leg to the position of the front one and dropping the front knee to nearly on the ground. Progress down the room in this manner, making the lunge punch with alternate hands as you go.

6. Take up the Straddle Leg Stance (Kiba Dachi) and remain in it for as long as you can at a time. Start with two minutes and work up to a quarter of an hour. This will strengthen the leg muscles.

7. To practise kicks, rest one hand against a wall to give yourself balance and practise raising the opposite leg as high as you can. Later try it without support from the wall.

8. Practise kicks to the front, trying to reach as high as possible. Do ten with each leg, then repeat until you have done enough.

9. To improve the height to which you can kick, let your partner take your foot and try to raise it gently until he can put it on his shoulder. Let him exercise both your legs in this way; then do the same for him.

10. To improve stamina, run. Karate students usually do so barefooted to toughen the soles of their feet, but use discretion about the nature of the ground so that you do not cut your feet. A few miles nightly will greatly improve your breathing, stamina and general health.

Index to Movements